NOT SUCH A BARGAIN

D1353971

NOT SUCH A BARGAIN

TOBY FORWARD

First published in Great Britain in 2012

Diffusion
an imprint of
SPCK
36 Causton Street
London SW1P 4ST
www.spckpublishing.co.uk

Reprinted with amendments 2014

ISBN 978-1-908713-00-1

Typeset by Graphicraft Ltd, Hong Kong
First printed in Great Britain by MPG Books
Subsequently digitally printed in Great Britain

Produced on paper from sustainable forests

Contents

1

Car boot

———•◦•———

Josh was glad it was a sunny day. He had his table set out and all the prices in place. Every Saturday morning he turned up at the car boot sale. If it rained it was hard work. A sunny day like today was best.

'Come on. Roll up. Get your bargains here,' he called out.

He leaned on the side of his old Ford van and smiled at everyone who walked past.

'How much is that?' asked a young woman. She held up a green vase.

Josh stood up and moved to her.

'To you, love, a fiver.'

She was almost as tall as Josh. He stood close to her and could smell her perfume. She looked about twenty. About the same age as him.

'I'll give you two pounds,' she said.

'Three and a kiss,' said Josh.

'I'd rather pay four pounds,' she said.

1

Josh pretended to be hurt. She was still smiling, joining in the joke.

He took the vase from her and looked at it.

'You can have it for three pounds,' he said, 'if you tell me your name.'

She looked at the other things on his table.

'You charge too much for your stuff,' she said.

Josh opened his hands.

'I only sell good stuff,' he said.

She put the vase back.

'Too much,' she said, and walked away.

Josh was about to run after her when a man said, 'How much is this?'

Josh sold him a lamp for seven pounds. And then it was too late. He looked for her but she didn't come back.

He put the green vase in the back of his van. Just in case.

Josh had a good day. He sold more than half of his stock and made over three hundred pounds. But all he could think about was the woman with the curly hair and the nice perfume.

By three o'clock most of the people had gone and it was time to pack up.

Josh sold some stuff off cheap, a chair and two pictures. It was better than putting it back in the van. He started to clear his table.

'Am I too late?'

Josh turned round and there she was. Green eyes, brown curly hair and a really good smile.

'Where have you been?' asked Josh.

'I was looking around. For a vase.'

She looked at Josh's table.

'Did you sell it? I can't see it.'

'Maybe,' said Josh.

She pulled a face.

'I really wanted that vase,' she said.

'You can still have it,' said Josh.

'How?'

'One pound,' said Josh.

He went to the van and got out the vase.

'OK,' she said. 'Thanks.'

'And your name,' said Josh.

The woman thought about it.

'Lisa,' she said.

Josh grinned.

'And a kiss,' he said.

Lisa took out two pounds.

'My name and two pounds,' she said. 'No kiss.'

Josh shook his head.

'One pound, your name and a kiss.'

Lisa shook her head this time.

'Take it or leave it,' she said.

She held out the coins.

'OK.'

Josh took the money and wrapped up the vase.

'Thanks, Lisa,' he said.

'Thank you.'

'Do you want to go out for a drink?'

'No,' said Lisa.

She walked away. Then, she looked over her shoulder and smiled.

'See you,' she called.

Things to think about . . .

Why does Josh put the vase in the back of his van?

Do you think Lisa likes Josh?

Why do you think Josh lets Lisa have her way?

2

Pay day

Josh kicked off his boots. He rubbed his feet. They were always sore after a day at the car boot.

He put the boots neatly under the bed and lay down.

Everything in Josh's room was neat and tidy. Not like the rest of the house.

He put his hands behind his head and looked up. He had a Spider-Man poster pasted to the ceiling. Kirsten Dunst in a web.

'Are you there, Josh?'

Josh sighed.

He had sneaked in. But his mum always knew. She was a bit deaf. She didn't hear him. But she always knew when he came home.

'Can I come in?' she called.

'Yes. Come on.'

She was tired. She was fifty and looked seventy. Josh blamed the fags. They always put years on you. But it was more than the fags. He knew that. It was years of hard work. It was worry. It was never having enough money. It was having a husband in prison.

Josh remembered visiting days when he was a boy. He was never allowed to go and see his dad. But visiting took it out of his mum. She was worried when she got up. She had a long bus ride to get there. Then there was the waiting. And nine times out of ten they had a row. And then she cried. And then his dad felt bad. And then she had the bus ride home. And then she fell asleep in front of the telly.

Josh would never forget visiting days. His dad was dead now. They died young in Josh's family.

'Did you have a good day?' she asked.

'Come on in,' said Josh.

His mum was hanging round the door. He swung his legs round and sat up on the bed.

'Sit here,' he said. She sat next to him.

He knew what she wanted.

'Well?' she said. 'Did you have a good day?'

'Two hundred and twenty pounds,' said Josh.

She looked at his things. The flat-screen television. The laptop. The sound system. The iPod. The wardrobe with his good clothes. The rows of Blu-ray Discs.

'That's good,' she said. 'Two hundred and twenty.'

He wanted her to ask him.

'Was it too hot?' she said.

'All right,' said Josh. 'I got a hat. And the van makes shade.'

She nodded.

He gave up. She never asked.

'Do you want some money?' he said.

His mum smiled at him.

'You were always a good boy,' she said.

He peeled some notes from his wad. Gave her a hundred.

'Too much,' she said. 'Not that much. Fifty will do.'

He put his hand on hers. He closed her fingers on the notes.

'Take it, Mum,' he said. 'I want you to.'

She leaned forward to kiss him. Josh turned away. She kissed his cheek.

'Thank you,' she said.

Josh smiled.

'I'm going out soon,' he said.

'Don't be late,' said his mum.

'Close the door after you,' he said.

He was twenty-three and she still treated him like he was a kid.

'Don't be late,' he said.

Things to think about . . .

What is Josh's room like?

What do you think the rest of the house is like?

What do you think Josh felt about his dad?

What do you think Josh wanted his mum to ask him?

3

The method

Monday morning bright and early Josh started work.

He liked an early start. Rain or sun it was all the same to him.

There were poor streets. There were rich streets. Sometimes Josh got more from the poor streets.

He had a cheerful smile. And the ladies liked his chat. The older ones liked it most.

'Got any rooms you want clearing?'

That was his best line. Nine times out of ten they did. The older women made him a cup of tea. They were lonely. They liked a chat. And he was good at the chat.

'I can help you out, ma,' he said. 'This room needs a bit of air.'

Before they knew it he was in his van and away. With chairs and pictures. With vases and bowls. With lamps and candlesticks. If he was out of luck he had to pay them. Not much. If he was lucky, they paid him.

'I'll take it all if you give me ten quid.'

Really good stuff he put on eBay. The rest went to the car boot.

Well, it helps them out, he said to himself. They need the space.

He didn't call it thieving. Not from the poor ones. Well, it wasn't. Not really. They helped him take the stuff away.

Even if they changed their minds and told the police, it was too late. He called himself Lee.

'Call me Lee, ma.'

He wrote his name and phone number out for them in case they wanted him. Only it was the wrong name. And if they rang the number they got a Chinese chip shop. The Chinese man was called Mr Lee. That made Josh laugh.

Josh had a different way with the rich houses.

He had a badge made. He wore it on a tape round his neck. It said he was on a scheme. For job seekers. But the only scheme he was on was his own.

'Any odd jobs you need done?' he would ask. About one in five let him in. They showed him a leaky tap. Or a loose floorboard. Or a cupboard door that was broken. He took out a little notebook and wrote some details.

'I can come back on Tuesday. I just need a washer.' Or a piece of wood. Or some glue. Or he had left his tools at home.

A cheeky smile often got him a cup of tea as well. Then he needed to use the toilet. It gave him lots of time. To steal a window key. To see what there was. Where the computer was. How big the sound system was. Any nice pieces for the car boot. He never took jewellery. It was too easy to identify. Often they had photographs of their rings and stuff. For the insurance. So he left it alone.

The best thing was the alarms. Most people forget their code. So they write it on a piece of paper by the control box. Once Josh had seen the code he was home and dry.

'When can I do it?'

'Not Thursday,' she would say. 'I'm having my hair done.' Or it would be, 'Not Wednesday, I'm going to see my mother.'

Easy. He knew where the stuff was. He knew what day the house was empty.

This was his method.

He never went at night. He wore a white overall and carried a toolbox. It was empty. Well, it was empty when he arrived, except for a hammer. It was full when he left.

Ring the bell. No answer? Good. Seeing her mum. Go round the back. Tap a hole in the window. Open it with the key. Get in quick. Punch in the code on the alarm. There you are.

Now he had all the time he needed to collect what he wanted. He opened the front door and carried the stuff out to the van. He usually whistled. No one expects a robber to whistle.

The good stuff went on eBay. The rest went to the car boot. Big stuff he shifted through a junk shop. They gave him bad prices. But all money is money.

Simple.

Anyway, today he did the poor streets. He got a good haul. One old man slammed the door in his face. That was bad. But you had to expect it. A couple of houses made him nervous. Sometimes they might call the police. But nothing bad happened. He got good results from four houses.

He paid one man five pounds for the lot. One woman gave him ten pounds to take it. And for two houses he did it for no cash either way.

In the last house, he took away an old biscuit tin. It had a picture of the Queen on it. And it had four hundred and twenty pounds in it.

Josh smiled when he opened it back home.

You should be more careful, ma, he said to himself.

The poor streets were often best. And easiest. But the rich ones were more fun. And more exciting.

He gave his mum an extra thirty quid at teatime.

Things to think about . . .

Is Josh clever?

What do you think of the way Josh works?

Why does Josh rob from the poor streets as well as the rich ones?

4

Special piece

Another Saturday. Another boot sale.

Josh put the stuff out on his table. It wasn't so sunny today. He liked a bit of cloud when he was selling. All the price tickets were in place. At one end of the table was a green bowl with a pattern of trees on it. He marked it at £500.

'You must be having a laugh,' said a man. 'Take five pounds for it.'

Josh shook his head.

'Special piece,' he said.

The man looked at it carefully.

'I know what this is worth,' he said. 'I collect pottery. This is never worth five hundred.'

'It is to me,' said Josh.

He knew the man was right.

Other people teased him about it as well. He just grinned and joked with them. As a matter of fact, he made more sales. Word went round about the five hundred pound bowl. They came to see it and then they bought something else.

Josh wished he had thought of it months ago.

Just before dinner-time Lisa turned up.

Josh couldn't keep the grin off his face. He wanted to act cool, but he was so pleased to see her. She was wearing the same perfume.

'Have you come back for another bargain?' he asked.

Lisa gave him a funny look.

'What are you playing at?' she said.

'What do you mean?'

She held out her green vase.

'I've brought this back,' she said.

'Do you want your money back?'

Josh was surprised.

'Yes, please,' she said.

'Is something wrong with it?' he asked.

'What do you think?'

She handed him the vase.

Josh looked at it. He turned it over. There was a mark on the bottom.

'No cracks,' he said. 'No chips. Worth what you paid.'

Lisa seemed angry.

'A friend came round and saw it. It's worth about four hundred pounds.'

'No way,' said Josh.

'Yes, it is,' said Lisa.

Josh whistled.

'Why did you bring it back?' he asked.

'Because I felt like a thief,' said Lisa. 'I only paid two pounds for it.'

'And a kiss,' said Josh.

'I never kissed you.'

'I thought you did.'

Josh knew that she hadn't given him the kiss. It was all part of the chat.

'If I had kissed you, you would remember,' said Lisa.

Josh tossed the vase from hand to hand.

'Be careful,' said Lisa.

'No,' said Josh. 'I think I kissed you. It was part of the deal.'

Lisa went red. Josh could see she was getting annoyed.

'No,' she said. 'There was no kiss.'

Josh leaned forward and she let him kiss her.
Not for long.

'Have you changed your mind about the drink?' he said.

'Perhaps.'

He handed the vase to her.

'No,' said Lisa. 'I can't afford it.'

Josh pressed it into her hands.

'It was a deal,' he said. 'You keep it.'

He picked up the bowl and gave her that as well.

Before she could stop him he kissed her again.

'A kiss, and you buy the first drink,' he said.

She pulled away and laughed.

'Eight o'clock, tonight,' said Josh. 'Do you know Bevan's Bar?'

'Of course.'

'See you there.'

Josh shook his head when she had gone. Some of these poor houses had better stuff than they knew. He should learn more about it.

Things to think about . . .

Do you think Lisa should trust Josh?

If Lisa were your friend, what would you say to her about Josh?

Does Josh know his business?

5

A very good kisser

———••••———

Monday morning again. Josh pulled off his T-shirt. He looked at himself in the mirror.

Not bad.

Not bad at all.

No need to go to the gym. All that carrying kept him fit.

You had to be trim for his work. In and out of houses. You had to be slim. Some of those windows were small.

He laughed. Proper Oliver Twist, he was. He broke into houses. And he always wanted more.

He wanted more of Lisa. That was for sure. Saturday night was great. She was cool and smart. She was pretty and sexy. You could be pretty and not sexy. You could be sexy and not pretty. She was both.

He took his shirt out of the wardrobe. His best shirt. It was the one he wore on Saturday. He put it to his face and breathed in. It smelled of Lisa. Her perfume.

18

Maybe he would never wash it. Maybe he would never wear it again.

No. Forget that.

He hung it up again.

Lisa.

He frowned.

He remembered Saturday night.

He asked her for her mobile number and she said no.

He asked her where she lived. She shook her head.

'How can I get in touch with you?' he asked.

She laughed.

'I can get in touch with you,' she said. 'If I want to.'

He gave her his number.

'I know where to find you,' she said. 'At the car boot.'

'I want to talk to you before then,' said Josh.

'Well, I think you can wait,' she said.

But she was a good kisser. A very good kisser.

He offered to take her home.

'No, thanks. A cab is good.'

'Do you want to go out again?' he asked.

'Maybe. Wait and see.'

All day Sunday he waited for her to ring him.

Nothing.

So now he had to go to work.

He kissed his mum on the way out. She put her arms round him. He hated it when she did that. He hated her clinging. She seemed so needy.

'Bye, Mum,' he called out. 'See you later.'

'Bye, love.'

Things to think about . . .

Why is Josh glad that he is fit?

Why does Josh like Lisa?

Why does Lisa like Josh?

6

Alarm

Josh got into the van and drove off. It always felt better when he was on the move.

The van was old and battered, but he loved it. He could be more alone there than anywhere else. It was better than being in his room. In the van his mum was never downstairs.

The only trouble was the tax. And the insurance. Two troubles, really. He had a licence, though. So he had to be careful. No boy-racer stuff at the lights. He drove like an old lady. Except you should see the way some of those old ladies drive.

He pulled into a pub car park and put on his white overalls and some thin latex gloves. Best to be ready. He knew the house he was going to. It was big and old. He liked old houses best. New ones had big windows and open lawns. Old houses had small windows. Old houses had gardens with trees and bushes. He liked a house you couldn't see from the road.

The van made a noise on the gravel in the drive.
That was good. Make a noise when you arrive.
It looks as though you should be there.

He slammed the van door. And he whistled, of
course. He got his toolbox from the back and
slammed that door as well.

There was no one in sight. The road had been quiet
as well. No one walking past. He strode up to the
front door and rapped the knocker. There was no
answer. He rapped again, louder. Still no answer.

Josh put his head to the door and listened.

'All right,' he shouted. 'Round the back? Great.'

This was in case anyone was looking. The house was
empty.

He walked round to the back. Empty. He looked in
the kitchen window. Empty. He put down his toolbox
and opened it.

'Leave it to me,' he called.

He took a hammer, smashed a piece out of the
window near the handle. It was the old type of
window. No locks. He opened it and jumped in.
He ran to the hall and found the alarm box.

'Oh, no!' he said. 'Where is it?'

He fumbled in his pocket.

Where was the code?

The green light flashed on the panel.

It was in his trousers. Josh grabbed the overalls and pulled them open.

The time was counting down.

He pushed his hand into his trouser pocket.

There it was.

The light turned to red.

Josh punched in 7 – 5 – 3 – 1.

The light turned back to green.

Josh sank to the floor and grinned. He was breathing fast.

Just in time.

Now the house was his.

Things to think about . . .

What risks does Josh take?

Are there too many?

Why does Josh rob houses?

7

Robbery with anger

It was the house Josh wanted. One day he would have one, just like this.

High ceilings. Three bathrooms. A kitchen as big as a football pitch. Well, nearly. A games room, with a full-size snooker table.

'Needs a swimming pool,' said Josh. He looked out at the garden. There was plenty of room for one.

He remembered the woman who lived here. She was old. At least fifty. And there were just the two of them. Her and her husband.

'The children come to stay,' she had told him. 'With their children. So we still need the space.'

Josh said he agreed with her. But he didn't. It was wrong. Two people in this big house. All alone. What right had they?

So he felt OK about taking some of their stuff.

Pity about the snooker table. He wished he could take that as well. It was all set up ready to play. The reds were in their neat triangle. Josh had to

do something about it. He took a cue and the
white. He crouched over the table and tried to
break off. He wanted a thin contact, just to brush
the pack. He drew back the cue and hit the white.
It missed the pack, bounced back and collided with
the yellow.

Josh swung the cue over his head. He smashed it
on the edge of the table. It broke in two. He pushed
the jagged edge across the cloth. It ripped with an
angry noise.

Josh threw the broken cue against the wall.

He was really annoyed.

He never got like this. He wondered what was
wrong with him.

He slammed out of the games room.

He made himself calm down. Even here noise
might attract attention. Best to be quiet. Best to
stick to the plan.

He found two big suitcases and filled them with
anything he liked the look of. There was plenty.
Royal Doulton china figures. Lead-crystal decanters.
Two laptops. Five clock radios. Who needed five
clock radios? One in every bedroom. A Blu-ray
and a DVD. A really good audio system from the
kitchen.

Josh worked faster than usual. He needed to burn off the anger. The cases were full when he stood in the master bedroom and took one last look.

There was a big jewellery box on the dressing-table. And some small boxes.

Josh never took jewellery.

It was too risky.

But these people had so much.

They deserved to lose it.

He could take it and throw it in the canal. Serve them right.

He made room for the boxes in one of the suitcases and got ready to go.

The van was right outside the house. He left the cases in the hall, took his toolbox and opened the front door. He stepped out, turned and shouted into the house.

'I'll back the van up. All right?'

He backed right up to the front door and loaded in the suitcases. No one could see what he was doing.

'Thanks a lot,' he called. 'See you this afternoon.'

He closed the door and drove off, well pleased. His anger had melted like ice in vodka.

Things to think about . . .

Did Josh lie to the owner about what he thought about the size of the house?

Is it less bad to steal from rich people than from poor people?

Should two people live in a house that big?

Do you think the lady 'deserves' to lose her jewellery?

8

Just this once

———◆◆◆———

Robbing made Josh hungry.

He took off the overalls and the gloves in the van before he drove away.

Straight for a burger.

He loved drive-thrus. It was like being in America.

Josh had never been to America. It was his dream. Sun and steaks. Disney and diners. The Wild West and the towering skyscrapers. It was all there.

He gave his order at the pod and drove up to the window.

'Dinner break?' the girl asked.

She must be bored. Sitting there handing out bags of burgers all day. What he did was better than that.

'Come and join me,' he said. He gave her his cheekiest grin.

'I wish,' she said.

He had to drive off. There were people behind him, waiting. Maybe he could come back and chat when they got quieter.

He slipped the clutch and blew her a kiss.

She made an offended face. Then she winked and grinned.

He still had it.

There was a small patch of waste ground by the canal. You had to drive past old warehouses to get to it. Josh went there and parked.

Lots of canals were clean now. You saw holiday boats on them. Not this one. This was dull and dirty. It oozed its brown way down the cut. Josh liked it better.

He chewed his burger and thought about the robbery.

He had liked the woman at first. She spoke to him nicely. It was only when he was alone in the house that he got angry. All that stuff. It wasn't fair.

The overalls were on the seat next to him. He wiped his fingers on them.

He checked the space around him. No other cars. No one walking. It wasn't a place for walking. Not clean. Not pretty. Not safe.

Josh got the boxes out of the case.

The big jewellery box had lots of old-looking stuff in it. Lots of it looked like it wasn't real. Costume stuff.

The real prizes were in the small boxes. He had seven of them. He could never sell this stuff. It would be traced. He didn't have the right sort of contact.

He sat back in his seat and thought about it.

He chose two boxes.

One had a brooch in it. It was gold, oval, with a band of pearls round the outside. His mum would like that.

And then in the biggest of the seven boxes there was a bracelet. Josh ran it through his fingers. It was lovely. Not too heavy, but plenty of it. Delicate links. It was as soft as a ribbon of silk. He put it on his wrist. It seemed to curl round his arm.

It would look great on Lisa.

And every girl loves gold.

It would be safe to keep them. It was only risky if you sold them. He could do it. Just this once.

Josh put those two boxes in the glove compartment. He took the others, and the big jewellery box, and he threw them into the canal.

Things to think about . . .

What does Josh think of women?

Is what Josh does better than selling burgers?

Why does Josh throw the jewellery away?

9

A surprise call

Tuesday. Josh's phone rang. He was sitting outside in the sun.

Number withheld.

Sales call probably.

He didn't answer those.

He was bored. The coffee was good. So was the muffin. The weather was fine. He watched the people hurrying past. Late for work. Going to a meeting. Catching a train. All busy. All tense. All under pressure. He was glad he wasn't them.

But he was still bored.

That was the thing about being a robber. You had a lot of spare time.

No one was his boss. No one told him what to do. He worked when he wanted to. He stopped when he felt like it. Two days a week were enough to keep the stall going and supply his eBay shop. Any more than two days and he would run out of streets to rob.

His phone beeped.

Voice mail.

That was odd. Sales calls don't leave messages.

Josh ran his spoon round the edge of his coffee cup to catch up the froth. He sucked the spoon. He let it clatter on the saucer. Might as well have another. Two was his limit now.

Three coffees would make him jumpy. He once had five coffees in one morning and picked a fight with the waiter.

Better check the phone.

He had to push his sunglasses away to see the screen. One voice message. He punched the buttons. Her voice broke into his morning. He smiled.

'Josh? This is Lisa. Look, I know it's short notice. I've got a free afternoon. Do you want to meet for lunch? I'll ring later.'

Yes!

Josh screwed round in his seat to look for the waiter. He saw his reflection in the coffee shop window. Great looks. Great style. How could she resist him? She couldn't. She had rung him. Result.

No time for another coffee. He paid the bill and went home.

'You're back early.'

'Hi, Mum. Yes. Can't stop.'

He took the stairs two at a time.

Another shower? Might as well. Two in one morning. He grinned. What if he got lucky? Another shower afterwards? Maybe together?

He dried off in the bedroom.

Change of clothes.

The phone rang while he was half dressed.

Number withheld.

'Yes?'

'Josh?'

'Hi, Lisa.'

'Did you get my message?'

'Yeah, that's fine.'

'You can do it?'

Josh looked at himself in the mirror. He flexed his shoulders, tilted his head to one side.

'Yes. I fixed it.'

'Sorry it was short notice.'

'No problem. I managed to get away.'

There was a pause.

Josh knew she was wondering what he got away from.

She didn't ask.

He spoke again before the silence closed in on them.

'What time?' he asked.

'One o'clock.'

'OK,' he said. 'I can do that. Where?'

'Do you know Carlo's? Off the main road.'

'I know it. See you there.'

He tossed the phone in the air and caught it. He spun round and looked at himself again. He pushed his best shirt to his face and drew in a deep breath. The perfume had faded. But it was still there. He put on a different shirt.

Ready to go.

One thing before he left.

He opened the door and called down.

'Mum.'

By the time she answered he was downstairs.

'Here,' he said.

He pushed a small box into her hand.

'Present for you.'

He gave her a quick kiss and ran out. Before she opened it.

Things to think about . . .

Is Josh better off than the people hurrying past?

Does Josh have too much time on his hands?

10

Lunch

———•◦•———

They agreed to have garlic bread.

'It's OK if we both do,' said Josh.

Lisa had olives as well.

Josh hated olives.

'I don't know how you eat them,' he said.

Lisa smiled.

She popped another olive in her mouth. Her
lips glistened. Josh wanted to lean forward and
kiss her.

'They never taste the same in England,' she said.

'What?'

'Olives. They taste best in Greece or Italy. Where
they grow them. With the sun on your neck. The
gleam of the sea. And the sky a blue you never see
in England.'

Josh tore off some garlic bread. He chewed it, then
took a big drink of red wine.

'What's the matter?' she asked.

'Nothing.'

'There is. What is it?'

'I've never been abroad.'

'Oh. I'm sorry.'

'Doesn't matter,' said Josh.

Lisa put out her hand and took his.

'I'm sorry,' she said.

He shrugged.

'What about when you were little? Didn't your parents take you away?'

Josh let her hold his hand. He said nothing.

'I'm making it worse,' she said. 'Talk about something else.'

'No,' said Josh. 'I don't mind. We didn't do those things. There was no money.'

'Look,' said Lisa. 'We don't have to talk about it if you don't want to. I don't mind.'

'Where did you go?' asked Josh. 'When you were a kid.'

Lisa looked embarrassed.

'Spain,' she said.

'And?' said Josh.

'France. Italy.'

'Your father's rich?'

'No. Just, you know, normal.'

The food came then. Josh was glad. It stopped them talking about holidays. By the time the plates were in front of them, they could talk about something else.

'What do you do?' asked Josh. 'For work.'

'In an office,' she said. 'There was a safety scare this morning. Something about air conditioning. Some fungus they found. They closed the office for the rest of the day.'

She leaned back and spread her hands and smiled.

'So, I'm here,' she said. 'Surprise.'

Josh couldn't stop himself from grinning.

'And you wanted to see me,' he said.

'Well,' said Lisa, 'all my friends are at work. I was at a loose end.'

Josh scowled.

Lisa gave his hand a light smack.

'Don't be daft,' she said.

'What?'

'All the others in the office have gone for a pub lunch. Then on to a film. I said I had things to do. I rang you. I wanted to see you, didn't I?'

Josh smiled again. His mood kept swinging. She made him excited and nervous. He wanted to please her. And he wanted her to like him.

It seemed the right time.

'Here,' he said. 'I brought this for you.'

He took out the long leather case and put it on the table.

'What is it?' she asked.

'Open it. Look and see.'

Lisa opened the case and saw the gold bracelet.

'You're joking,' she said.

'No.'

Lisa took out the bracelet. She draped it on her wrist.

Josh loved the way it followed the curve of her arm.

'It looks lovely,' he said.

'Is it real?'

'Course it is.'

She put it back in the box.

'I can't take it.'

She pushed the box back to him.

'What?'

'I can't take it. It's too much. Too expensive.'

'So?'

'I don't know you,' she said.

'Get to know me,' said Josh.

She shook her head. Her chicken was half finished. She pushed it away.

'I have to go,' she said.

'No. Stay here. Please. What's the matter?' asked Josh.

Lisa gave him a hard look.

'Where does this money come from?' she asked. 'You had no money for holidays. Now you give me a gold bracelet. And a vase worth four hundred pounds. Where does it come from? What do you do? Tell me, or I don't want to see you again.'

Things to think about . . .

How does Josh feel when Lisa talks about her holidays abroad?

Do you think Josh is as confident as he sounds?

Why do you think Lisa makes him feel 'excited and nervous'?

11

In the park

———•◦•———

Josh wouldn't speak to Lisa. He got the bill and paid it.

'I'm paying half,' she said.

'No. It's on me.'

Lisa put the money on the table. She stood up and walked away. Josh had to settle with the waiter. When he got out she was there. She had waited. He nearly fell over with relief.

'Talk to me. Or I'm gone,' she said.

'Not here. Come on,' said Josh.

They walked in silence to the park. Josh found a bench and sat down. Lisa moved away a little. It was high up and they could see the river.

'What does your dad do?' asked Josh.

'It's not about me,' said Lisa.

'Yes, it is. What does he do?'

'He works in a bank. What about your dad?'

'My dad's dead.'

Lisa looked uncomfortable.

'I'm sorry,' she said.

'Doesn't matter. I didn't really know him anyway.'

'What was his job?'

'He didn't have one.'

They sat in silence. The river never seemed to move. The ferry crossed half way before either of them spoke again.

'Look, I'm sorry about your dad,' she said. 'But I need to understand. Do you make a living at the car boot? You can't, can you?'

The silence had given Josh time to think.

'I'm a trader,' he said. 'Car boot. eBay. It's enough to keep me.'

'All right,' said Lisa. 'That makes sense. Where does the stuff come from?'

Josh was ready with his answer.

'House clearance.'

'What's that?'

Josh leaned forward, to convince her.

'People die,' he said. 'The relatives live a long way away. They need to sell the house. Or they do a flit and the landlord wants it cleared. Or they can't pay the mortgage. I don't know. Lots of reasons. Anyway, that's where I come in. I get a call. I take the van round. They pay me to clear it and I keep whatever's there.'

'Everything?' said Lisa. 'Like a gold bracelet. I don't think so.'

'That's the thing,' said Josh. 'Sometimes the relatives clear what they want first. And they miss things. Sometimes they think there's nothing good. They don't even come up to look. I take some stuff to the tip. But there isn't much you can't sell. Some stuff is really good. The bracelet. That vase you bought.'

She looked doubtful.

He laughed. 'You've seen the stall at the car boot. The things some people will pay money for.'

He put his hands behind his head and looked at her. He was holding his breath. Trying to look casual.

She paused and looked at him.

'So you didn't buy it for me? Someone just left it and you got paid to take it away?'

Josh swore silently. He hadn't seen that coming. Now he looked cheap. He tried to explain. Lisa linked her arm through his.

'It's OK. I'm only joking. I just don't ever want anything that's stolen. You understand?'

Josh relaxed. She was buying it.

'Don't you think,' said Lisa, 'you should tell the family?'

'What?'

'If you find something valuable. You should tell them.'

Josh sighed.

'It's business,' he said. 'They agree and pay me to take it. Legally, it's mine.'

'Legally it is,' she agreed. 'But morally?'

Josh didn't want to go there. He was half believing his own story till then. Morally and legally it was all nicked.

'Are we OK?' he asked.

She thought about it.

'Maybe,' she said. 'But I'm not keeping the bracelet. It doesn't feel right.'

She squeezed his arm.

'When can I see you again?' asked Josh.

'Soon as you like,' said Lisa. 'Any Sunday you're working.'

'What do you mean?'

'I'm coming with you,' she said. 'On a clearance job.'

'Are you checking up on me?'

Lisa smiled. 'I just want to help.'

She kissed his cheek.

'My van's broken down.'

'I'll wait. You'll have to get it mended. Or you'll go out of business.'

This was so bad. It was all going wrong.

'Come out Friday night.'

'No. I'll ring you Friday and see you Sunday. If you're working. If the van's fixed.'

'I don't work Sundays.'

'Monday then. I'll pull a sickie. I'll come any day you tell me.'

'It's not easy,' said Josh.

'You won't believe how easy it is,' she said. 'If you want to see me again, you'll have to take me on a job.' She stood up to go.

Josh stood up as well. 'Stay a bit longer,' he said. 'Talk about it.'

'I'm going,' she said. 'I'll ring you.'

She turned to face him. She put her arms around him and kissed him.

'That's it,' she said.

She stood back and smiled. He had never seen anything so lovely.

'See you,' she said. 'Whenever you're ready.'

Josh watched her walk away and he groaned.

Things to think about . . .

Why does Lisa insist on paying half?

What do you think about the story Josh gives about how he works?

Do you think there is a difference between 'legally' and 'morally'?

Does Lisa believe the story?

12

Bingo

———•◦•———

His mum was getting ready to go out.

'You're back early,' she said.

'Nice day,' said Josh. 'I'm taking some time out.'

She came and gave him a hug. He tried to wriggle away.

'Don't do that, Josh-boy.'

She looked hurt.

He let her hug him and even let her give him a kiss.

'You're a good boy,' she said.

'Mum,' he complained.

'Oh, I know,' she said. 'You're all grown up, but you're still my boy.'

She stood back.

'Look,' she said.

She was wearing the brooch.

'You like it?' he asked.

'I love it. You're a good boy.'

She came towards him, for another hug. He gave her a quick kiss on the cheek.

'You off to bingo?' he asked.

'I'll win our fortune,' she said. 'You won't have to work again.'

He was on the stairs now. Out of reach.

'You enjoy yourself,' he said.

'What will you do?'

He shrugged.

'See you,' he called as she shut the door.

Things to think about . . .

Why does Josh try to keep his distance from his mum?

Is Josh a 'good boy'?

How would things change if his mum did win a fortune at bingo?

13

A warning

The sun was shining. The day was warm. He was free to go where he wanted. It was a day for walking in the country. Lying on a beach. Sitting in the garden. So he went to the betting shop.

Not one of your big bookies. They were all thieves. He went to Mick's. Mick was all right. He had a betting shop in the street. And on local race days he took his bag to the course.

Josh left the bright sun behind. Mick's was dismal and scruffy. The floor was littered with losing betting slips. There were coffee rings on the counters. No smoking inside. But it blew in from the pavement. People hardly left to light up. One foot inside, one foot outside. The dog-ends littered the entrance. Smell of smoke and sweat. Heaven. Josh was at home. Sun was all right. But Mick's was better.

'All right there, Josh?' Mick called.

Not a local race day.

'What's the matter, Mick?' asked Josh. 'Someone died?'

Mick put his finger to his lips. He spoke to the woman next to him. She was about forty. Looked like a fat nurse. Friendly but no nonsense.

'Look after it for ten minutes, Chris,' said Mick.

'All right,' she said. 'How are you, Josh?'

'All the better for seeing you,' he said, and winked.

She laughed.

'I should be so lucky,' she said. 'Go on. Get out.'

Mick punched the security code on the door and came out.

'I'll buy you a cup of tea,' he said.

'Bloody hell, Mick,' said Josh. 'Are you feeling ill?'

Chris laughed again.

'Make sure he pays,' she called.

There was a cafe three doors down. They got a corner table. Mick ordered the teas and picked them up. He left Josh to pay.

'What's up?' asked Josh.

Mick leaned forward. His arms were on the table.

'Police,' he said.

'What?'

Josh's head felt light. He didn't want to hear this.

'You been doping the horses?' he joked.

'Don't muck about,' said Mick.

'What then?'

'They've been asking about stolen goods.'

Josh looked out of the window. As if they were there.

'So?' he asked. 'You don't go robbing, do you?'

'Don't muck about,' said Mick. 'The thing is, in the past, I might have had some stuff.'

'What do you mean?'

'You know. A punter can't afford a bet. He offers me his watch, so I take it. Or his wife's ring. You know. I give a value. If he wins, he wins. If he loses, I keep it.'

'No harm in that.'

'Well, there was,' said Mick. 'No paperwork. You know. Taxman doesn't like that.'

'Right.'

'And sometimes, not now. But sometimes. It wasn't really his wife's ring. You understand me.'

Josh liked this less and less.

'Did you go down?'

Mick finished his tea.

'Look, Josh. I don't like doing this. All right?'

'Go on.'

'I gave them some names. People to look at. People who brought me good things. You understand? It was all a long time ago.'

'You grassed them up?'

Mick stood up.

'I'm doing you a favour, Josh. All right? The police turned a blind eye then. I got lucky. I don't do it any more.'

'Why are you telling me this? I pay cash, don't I?'

'Yes, you do,' said Mick. 'Every time. The thing is, where does the cash come from, Josh?'

Josh stood up and faced him.

'Don't tell me. I'm not asking,' said Mick. 'I'm just saying. That's all.'

'What did you say to the police?'

'Nothing. I don't need to. I'm clean. But they're asking around. OK?'

'You grassed them up,' said Josh.

'I did what I had to,' said Mick. 'And I'm telling you now, because of your dad.'

'What?'

'He was a friend of mine. So I'm giving you a word. That's all. The police are asking. Round here. For jewellery that's been stolen.'

Josh sat down again.

'Think about it,' said Mick. 'All right?'

Josh watched Mick go. The sun bounced off the sauce bottles.

Things to think about . . .

What do you think about Mick's shop?

Why does Josh ask Mick if he is feeling ill?

Mick says, 'I'm telling you because of your dad.' What do you think he means?

14

Police

Josh needed time to think. He ordered the all-day breakfast.

'No black pudding,' he said. 'And fried bread instead of hash browns.'

'Coming up. More tea?'

'Please.'

Josh made a picture of his bedroom in his head.

The TV was nicked. So was the Blu-ray. The computer was OK. He'd bought that. All the clothes were OK. He didn't wear other people's stuff. The clock radio would have to go.

By the time he had eaten he had it all sorted in his head. What had to go. What could stay. He could load it into the van and dump it in the canal.

Best do it straight away.

'Thanks,' he called. 'Good breakfast.'

'Cheers.'

His mum was still at bingo. He backed up the van
to the house. The TV went in first. It left a big gap
on the wall. Then the Blu-ray. He slipped the bracelet
box into his pocket. He'd throw that in as well. Tell
Lisa he'd sold it. Buy her something instead.

He locked the van and went into the house. Better
leave his mum a note. She might go into his
bedroom. She'd think they'd been robbed. What if
she called the police? That made him laugh. He was
still laughing when there was a knock at the door.

It was the police. That stopped him laughing.

'What do you want?'

'Can we come in?'

There were two of them. They always come in twos.

'No,' said Josh.

'Only for a minute.'

'What for?'

'Just a chat,' said one.

'And a look around,' said the other.

Josh wanted to slam the door on them. He had
never had trouble with the police. He hated himself
for being frightened now.

'Nothing to worry about. If you've got nothing to
hide,' said one.

'What's this about?' he demanded.

He stepped outside and closed the door.

The policemen looked at each other.

The taller one pointed at the van.

'Is that your van?' he asked.

'No.'

'It's outside your house.'

'So are you. Does that make us married?' asked Josh. 'Cause you're not my type.'

'So it's not your van?'

Josh was going red. He was no good at lying.

'We can ask around,' said the other one.

'There's no tax, you see,' said his colleague.

'It's not mine,' said Josh.

'You'll need your keys,' said the tall one. 'To get in the house. Can we see them?'

The van key was on the key-ring.

'I'm not going in,' said Josh.

'We'll wait till you do.'

'Here,' shouted a loud voice. 'What's going on here?'

Josh groaned silently. It was his mum. This would upset her. He might as well own up. To protect her.

'It's all right, love,' said the tall copper. 'Just move away.'

Things to think about . . .

What do you think of Josh's plan to dump the stuff?

Josh 'hated himself for being frightened'. Is he right to hate himself for that?

What do the police think of Josh?

What would have happened if Josh's mum hadn't turned up?

15

Mum

———•◦•———

She was wearing the brooch.

The policeman looked down at her.

The brooch looked up at him.

He couldn't miss it.

'Do you live here?' he asked.

'Course I do. Now push off.'

'Is that your van?'

He pointed to Josh's van. This was it. It was all over. They'd look in the van and he'd be arrested. He felt the weight of the bracelet in his pocket. That would come out when they searched him.

'What van?' she said.

'That van.'

It was right outside her house. There was no other van in sight.

'That van?' she asked.

'Yes.'

'The white one?'

'Yes.'

'Never seen it before.'

Josh stared at her.

'It's not taxed,' said the policeman.

'So?'

'That's an offence.'

'So?'

'Look, ma,' he began.

'Don't you "ma" me, lad. What do you want?'

'There've been burglaries.'

'What's that got to do with us?'

Josh was amazed. He'd never seen his mum like this.

The other one, the smaller one, stepped in.

'We were tipped off to come here,' he said. 'We want to look inside the house.'

'You got a warrant?'

'No.'

'Sod off, then. Understand? Get out of here.'

She put her hand on the tall one's chest and pushed.

He backed away. She kept walking and he kept backing away.

'Go on. Get. Clear off.'

And they did. Josh and his mum watched them all the way up the road.

'Bloody hell, Mum,' he said. 'How did you do that?'

He bent to give her a kiss on the cheek. She pushed him away.

'What?' he asked.

'I had enough of this with your dad,' she said. 'Don't you come round me now. I won't have it.'

Josh nodded.

'What do you have to do?' she asked.

'Drive the van off,' said Josh. 'Dump some stuff.'

'Do it quick then. Before they come back,' she said. 'They'll have a warrant next time.'

'I'll go now.'

'You got everything?'

Josh paused.

She sighed and shook her head.

'Do you need this?' she asked.

'Yes,' said Josh.

She took off the brooch.

'Pity,' she said. 'It's nice.'

'Sorry.'

'Doesn't matter.'

Josh drove off and headed for the canal.

He ditched the stuff.

The black water gurgled, shifted and settled.

All that money.

Drowned.

It was hard throwing the bracelet in. And the brooch.

Part of him felt sorry for the woman he stole them from. Part of him was angry to lose them.

He left the keys in the van.

The van could stay there. With the door open.

Someone would nick it. Or torch it. It would be gone by night-time.

He got a bus home. It dropped him at the end of the road.

There was a car outside the house. Unmarked police car. Stood out a mile.

He pushed open the front door. A uniformed copper was in the kitchen.

'What's up?' he asked.

'We've been burgled,' said his mum. 'The police are in your room.'

Things to think about . . .

The police say they were 'tipped off'. Who tipped them off?

What do you think about the way Josh's mum handles the police?

Should Josh's mum say more to Josh?

How do you think Josh feels about dumping his van?

16

A nice cup of tea

———•◦•———

Had he forgotten anything? He took the stairs two at a time. He thought the room was clean. Maybe he had something else?

His room door was open. There were two in there. Plain clothes. Wearing those latex gloves. Like the ones he wore for robbing.

One of them was holding the biscuit tin with a picture of the Queen on it. He was a fat-faced copper. His mate was bald and looked strong.

'Hello, Josh,' said Fat-face. 'What's this?'

It was the tin with four hundred pounds in. He had taken it from the old woman.

'It's mine,' said Josh.

Fat-face opened it. He smiled.

'Oh, look,' he said. 'Money.'

The bald one came and stood right up close to Josh. Threatening.

'Where did you nick it from?' he asked.

'It was from his nan,' said Josh's mum. She was standing by the door.

'What? He nicked it from his nan?'

'She gave it to him.'

Fat-face looked disappointed.

'Why?'

'Because she loves him. Because he's a good boy. Aren't you, Josh-boy?'

She patted Josh's cheek. He was very red-faced.

Fat-face tried to smile, but it didn't work.

'Now bugger off,' she said. 'And find the sod who broke in and did this.'

Josh and his mum watched them leave the house.

'Did you do that?' asked Josh.

'Do what?'

'Trash my bedroom.'

'Let's have a nice cup of tea,' she said.

'Did you?'

'Course I did. It always works. It puts the cops on the back foot, and it destroys evidence.'

'Mum!' said Josh.

She poured the water on the tea bags.

'Don't you "Mum" me,' she said. 'I learned a few tricks from your dad.'

She looked very serious now.

'But I don't want all that again. Not with you. Not prison.'

Josh looked away.

'I can't do that again,' she said. 'The visiting. Being treated like dirt. Queuing up. Don't make me do that.'

Josh tried to change the subject.

'That was brilliant,' he said. 'About the tin, with the money in it.'

She grinned. Just for a second. Then she looked sad.

'She wouldn't mind,' she said. 'Rest her soul.'

She handed Josh a mug of tea.

'But,' she added, 'it was some old lady's, wasn't it?'

Josh didn't answer.

'Some old lady. Just like your nan,' said his mum. 'It was her savings.'

Things to think about . . .

What do you think of the way Josh's mum handles
the situation?

Why do you think Josh's mum hasn't said
anything to him before?

Is Josh's mum worried about Josh, or herself?

Does thinking that the money belonged to
someone's nan make it different?

17

Hiding place

———◆·◆·◆———

Josh couldn't believe he'd got away with it.

The police knew. They must have known. It was obvious. But they couldn't say anything.

'Think they'll come back again?' asked Josh.

'Not for a bit,' she said.

Josh looked at her in admiration.

'I've never seen you like this,' he said.

'You've never had to before. Don't let it happen again.'

'I promise,' he said. 'I told you already.'

'There's something else,' she said.

'What?'

'You know.'

'What?' Josh asked again.

His mum tapped the side of his face.

'You wouldn't last five minutes on your own,' she said. 'In a police station. Go and get it.'

Josh went upstairs again. He went to the wardrobe in his mum's room. There was a shelf at the top. He moved some scarves and jumpers to one side. There was nothing there. Josh climbed on a chair and looked right at the back. Nothing. Just more clothes.

He ran downstairs.

His mum was still at the kitchen table.

There was a parcel in front of her. Brown paper. Tied with string.

Josh felt himself go red.

'You looking for this?' she asked.

She pushed it across the table to him.

'How much is in there?' she asked.

Josh didn't answer.

'I want to know,' she said.

'Seventeen thousand pounds,' said Josh.

'And you hid it in my wardrobe?' she said. 'First place they looked, after they started on your room. I took it out before they got here.'

Josh looked away from her.

'Take it,' she said. 'Go on. I don't want it in the house.'

'Where did you hide it?' he asked.

'Never mind that.'

She was starting to wind down. The fierce look was going. She looked old again. Tired. And hurt.

'I'm sorry, Mum,' said Josh. 'It was stupid.'

She nodded.

'It was,' she said. 'But it was cruel as well.'

'What?'

'You involved me, Josh. You used my bedroom for it. I don't want that.'

'I'm sorry,' he said again.

'I know you are. It's all right. But get rid of it.'

'I will,' said Josh. 'But where did you hide it?'

She smiled, and she was young again.

'On the table. In the living room. They walked straight past it and up the stairs. It always works.'

'You're joking,' said Josh.

'No. I was banking on getting rid of them before they noticed it.'

She leaned forward.

'They think we're stupid. Hiding things in wardrobes. Dropping them in cisterns. Under the mattress. They were too busy looking in cupboards to look on the bloody table.'

Josh took the parcel.

'Are you going then?' she asked. 'I don't want it in the house.'

Josh didn't move.

She sighed.

'You don't know what to do, do you?' she said.

Josh felt like he was ten years old again.

'I'd better throw it in the canal,' he said.

'What?'

He shrugged.

'It's useless,' he said. 'I can't put it in the bank. I can't spend it. I can't hide it anywhere. It's all money laundering these days. Cash is no good.'

She shook her head.

'What are you like?' she said.

Josh started to feel angry with her now.

'You don't know,' he said. 'If I try to spend a pile of cash anywhere they'll call the police. I can keep maybe two, maybe three thousand. From the car boot. The rest is rubbish.'

He stood up.

'I'll get rid of it,' he said. 'Do you want a couple of hundred first?'

His mum looked hard at him.

'Listen,' she said. 'This is what you have to do. Go and see Mick the Bookie.'

'What?' said Josh. 'What can he do?'

She explained it to him.

'Do you think it will work?' he asked.

'Yes.'

'Will he do it?'

She stared at him.

'Tell him I sent you,' she said.

Things to think about . . .

How does Josh feel when he thinks his life savings have been taken?

How do you think the old lady felt when she couldn't find her biscuit tin?

What do you think Josh has learned from his mum?

Has your view of Josh's mum changed?

18

Payment time

————•—•—————

Mick looked nervous when Josh went in.

'No hard feelings,' said Mick.

There were only three punters in the shop.

'You're quiet,' said Josh.

'Not worth opening the shop,' said Mick.

Josh smiled.

'I've never met a poor bookie,' he said.

'You have now,' said Mick. 'I'm struggling.'

'Let's go for a drive,' said Josh.

'I'm busy.'

'Chris can take care of it. Can't you, Chris?'

Chris looked at Mick.

'It's important,' said Josh. 'And we need to be private.'

Mick nodded.

'The car's round the corner,' said Mick.

'I know,' said Josh. 'Out of sight of the customers. You poor bookie.'

Mick shrugged.

It was a short walk to the car. A new BMW, fully loaded.

'My heart bleeds for you,' said Josh.

'Get in,' Mick ordered.

Josh had never even been in a room as luxurious as the inside of the Beamer. He didn't think he'd ever sat in a seat that comfortable.

'Where to?' asked Mick.

'Doesn't matter. Just drive.'

Mick stayed close to the area. He drove round and back again in loops.

'What do you want?' he said.

'I just won seventeen thousand pounds,' said Josh.

Mick nearly drove off the road.

'How much?'

Josh told him again.

'Who from?' asked Mick.

'You.'

Mick pulled in to the side of the road. He turned to look at Josh.

'Are you being funny?' he asked.

'Am I laughing?' asked Josh.

He took the parcel out of his backpack.

'Here you are,' he said.

Mick ignored him.

'Take it,' said Josh.

'Stop pissing about,' said Mick.

Josh undid his seat belt.

'I'm getting out,' he said. 'And I'm leaving this here.'

'Why? I don't want it. Take it with you.'

Josh spoke carefully.

'There's seventeen thousand pounds in there,' he said. 'Today I'm making a bet with you, for one hundred pounds. I will win. Long odds. And tomorrow I will make a bigger bet. With the winnings.'

'No,' said Mick. 'Forget it.'

'In three days,' said Josh, 'I'm going to win four thousand pounds. I'll come and collect it. Over the next month I'm going to win seventeen thousand pounds. All right?'

'I can't,' said Mick.

'You'll have to.'

'There's paperwork. Tax. Receipts. It isn't possible.'

'Sort it,' said Josh.

Mick pushed the parcel at Josh.

'Why should I?' he asked.

Josh didn't want to say the next thing. But he had to. It hurt his pride. But it was the only way.

'Because my mum says you owe her,' he said. 'And you owe me. Understand?'

Josh stepped out of the car.

Mick put his hand on the parcel.

'And then we're quits,' he said.

'Then we're quits,' Josh agreed.

Things to think about . . .

Why does Mick look nervous when he sees Josh?

What do you think about the plan? Is it fair on Mick?

Could Josh have kept his money without involving someone else?

Why does Mick owe Josh and his mum?

19

Adverts

Josh had a happy three days.

He walked a lot.

The streets looked different now he wasn't in the van.

It was slower. Closer. The people were more real. He felt more like them.

He remembered houses he had visited. People he had cheated. And most of them still didn't know. He'd told them they got a good deal from him. And they had believed him.

It made him think.

He drank a lot of coffee as well. He liked sitting alone, watching people. The coffee shops were always busy. No one seemed to go to work any more.

And he thought a lot.

He thought about Lisa.

He was pretty sure he would see her again.

Probably.

It was a nice feeling. Not having to lie to her now.

He looked at the paper as well.

Not the news. He didn't care much about the news.

He looked at the adverts.

For sale.

Wanted.

People wanted the strangest things.

Someone wanted a garden swing.

Someone wanted a food mixer, but it had to be a certain one.

Someone wanted a dog collar with seven studs.

Why seven?

People sold the strangest things.

Someone was selling a canoe with no paddle.

Someone was selling a cot. Never used.

Someone was selling five hair dryers.

Who has five hair dryers?

A thief, that's who.

Josh thought the police might be answering that advert.

Stupid prat.

And there were vans for sale.

Josh needed a van. And soon he would have the money to buy one. He noted some phone numbers and addresses.

Then he found another number. The newspaper. He keyed it into his mobile.

'Hello,' he said. 'I want to put an advert in the paper.'

He got through to the right person. She helped him to work out the right words.

'Every day,' said Josh. 'From now on, please.'

She told him what it would cost. Less than he thought.

'I'll come round with the money,' he promised. 'In an hour.'

Things to think about . . .

Why does Josh feel happy?

Do you think Josh will see Lisa again?

Why does Josh need a new van?

20

Van

Then Josh sorted his room out.

He'd need a new flat-screen. But not yet. So he hung some pictures instead. He moved the furniture round. With no telly the room looked bigger. He liked that.

The next morning he looked at vans.

The best one was a thousand pounds more than he was getting from Mick for the first payment.

'Sorry,' said Josh. 'I need the van next week, but I'm short. I can't pay all of it for another two weeks. Thanks, anyway.'

The man selling looked at Josh.

'Will you bring the other thousand in two weeks?' he asked.

Josh was surprised.

'Will you trust me?' he asked.

The man thought about it.

'You look honest,' he said. 'OK. It's a deal.'

They shook hands on it.

'I'll come back tomorrow,' said Josh. 'With a cheque. Will you take that?'

'All right.'

Josh felt sick when he walked away. There was a park round the corner. He went there and sat down. A wind was picking up. The trees bent and sniggered at him.

He could have the van for a thousand less. Give him the cheque and walk away. The man would never get the rest. Easy.

'You look honest,' the man had said.

Josh leaned back and took deep breaths.

On the way home he made a detour. He called in at Mick's.

'Tomorrow,' said Mick. 'You said tomorrow.'

'That's right,' said Josh. 'I'll be here then. But make it five, not four. All right?'

He slid a piece of paper across the counter. It had a name on it.

'Make it out to him,' he said.

Mick started to argue, but Josh walked out. He didn't listen.

Things to think about . . .

The man selling the van thinks Josh looks honest. How does Josh feel about that and why?

Does Josh do the right thing?

If you were a friend of Mick's, what would you think of Josh?

21

In his own name

———•••———

Josh went home and logged on to his computer. He closed his eBay shop. Best not to leave any traces. Most of the stuff he sold was nicked.

There wasn't a lot. He didn't like the risk. And it was in his mum's name. He felt ashamed of that now. He had a credit card account in her name. She didn't know about it. All done by him. Best not to tell her.

He could open his own bank account next week. With a proper cheque from Mick. All above board. Then he'd start again with eBay. In his own name.

He shut the eBay window. All done.

He clicked a porn site.

Too loud. He killed the sound.

It just made him think of Lisa.

That didn't feel good.

He logged off.

He could hear his mum laughing at the telly.

His room was too small. No air. He needed to get out.

Josh rattled down the stairs.

'Bye, Mum,' he shouted.

He slammed the front door before she had time to answer.

He wanted to see Lisa. If he knew where she lived, he'd go round. Just to be near the house. He took out his phone and looked at it. As if looking would make her ring him.

He couldn't keep his hands still.

He texted Jay. A mate he hadn't seen for ages.

'Where u now?'

There was hardly a pause before his phone beeped.

'Angel. U cummin?'

Josh hit the buttons.

'CU in 10.'

Josh should have guessed. Jay was always at the Angel. He spent more time there than at home.

Jay was alone at the pool table when Josh arrived.

'Want another?' Josh called.

'Cheers,' said Jay.

Josh bought two pints. He gave one to Jay.

'Game?' asked Jay.

Josh slid a pound coin into the slot.

Jay racked the balls.

'You working?' asked Josh.

'Don't make me laugh.'

Jay broke and sank a stripe.

'You ever worked?' asked Josh.

Jay sank another.

'I'll work with you if you like,' he said. Jay didn't even look up when he said it.

Josh didn't answer.

Jay missed his shot and Josh cued up.

'What help would you be?' he asked Jay. 'You don't know what I do.'

Josh missed his spot and stood away from the table.

Jay chalked his cue.

'I could help you carry stuff,' he said. 'And I could keep watch.'

He looked at Josh when he said this. To let him know that he knew what Josh did.

'Play your shot,' said Josh.

They didn't speak again till the game was over.

Jay won.

'Loser pays,' said Jay.

Josh slid another coin in.

He racked the balls.

'I'll give you a job,' he said at last.

Jay looked astonished.

'You serious?' Jay asked.

'Are you?' said Josh.

Jay hesitated.

'Yeah,' he said. 'Why not? I can keep my mouth shut.'

'Why would you do that?' asked Josh.

'Police,' said Jay.

Josh laughed. 'You call that keeping your mouth shut?' he said.

Jay finished his pint.

'Here's the deal,' said Josh. 'You start Monday. Nine o'clock. I'll pick you up. All right?'

'Sorted,' said Jay.

'You work one month, half pay. On trial,' said Josh.

'What? I can't do that. What will I live off?'

'Same as you always do,' said Josh. 'The Social. Call it work experience. Or an apprenticeship.'

Jay shook his head.

'You're having a laugh,' he said.

'No,' said Josh. 'Serious. If you're any good I'll take you. I'll pay you twice what you get on the Social. Up to you.'

Jay broke off the pack.

'All right,' he said. 'Do I need anything?'

'Come casual,' said Josh. 'Ready for some hard work.'

Jay shook his head.

'Do I need a mask, or anything?' he asked.

Josh leaned on his cue.

'Don't be such a prat,' he said.

Things to think about . . .

Why does Josh feel ashamed about his eBay shop?

How has Josh's attitude to his mum changed? Why?

If you were a friend of Josh's, would you say it was a good idea to take on Jay?

22

Work

It worked.

Mick gave Josh the cheque.

Josh gave it to the man.

Two phone calls and he was taxed, insured and on the road.

Legit.

'Cost of insurance,' said Josh. 'It's worse than robbery.'

'Tell me,' said the man.

He waved him off.

And there were other calls. Incoming. The advert was working. Josh made times and dates. And he made promises.

Josh went to the car boot late on Saturday. He didn't take the van. Nothing to sell. But he stayed most of the rest of the day. Looking for Lisa. She didn't turn up.

It was starting to rain when Josh left.

He'd given her up when his phone beeped a message.

'Want to meet nxt wk? Lisa. X'

And there was a number.

He punched in a fast reply.

'Tuesday?'

It took her ages to reply.

'OK. Where? When?'

Josh didn't text back. He rang the number. It rang out. Then went to voice mail.

He swore.

His thumbs moved over the keys.

'Y don't u ansr?'

No reply. He stared at the phone.

What was she doing to him?

He texted a time and place for Tuesday.

'CU there,' she texted back. 'Can't w8. X'

Neither could Josh. But he had to.

He went to Jay's house on Monday morning.

'You can't come like that,' said Josh. 'I said casual. For work.'

'Is this your van?' said Jay.

He kicked a tyre.

'Get changed,' said Josh. 'It isn't a party.'

Jay scowled.

'Go on,' said Josh.

'I haven't had breakfast,' said Jay.

'Ten minutes,' said Josh. 'And then I'm going without you. No job. No cash. Understand?'

Jay looked at Josh's clothes. Jeans. Boots. T-shirt and jacket.

'All right.'

It took him nine minutes.

Josh already had the engine running.

Jay was wearing the same as Josh. He jumped in the cab.

'Toast?' he said.

He had two slices. One of them half eaten.

Josh shook his head.

'Can we stop for coffee?' asked Jay.

'No time,' said Josh.

'Only take-out,' said Jay. 'I'll buy you one.'

Josh pulled up outside a Costa. On a yellow line.

'Make it quick,' he said. 'Double espresso. Hot milk on the side.'

Jay grinned at him. He wiped his fingers on his shirt.

'Sorted,' he said.

Ten minutes later they were at the first house.

Josh turned off the engine.

'Do as you're told,' he said to Jay. 'And don't nick anything. Or you're dead.'

'Whatever,' said Jay.

Josh took a deep breath and knocked on the door. A lady opened it. Grey hair. Sensible shoes.

'Hello, love,' said Josh. 'House clearance. You rang and booked.'

'That's right,' she said. 'Come on in.'

They did all right.

It was hard work. Jay was slow at first. And he complained. But he got the hang of it. He even enjoyed it.

They stopped for lunch.

'This is all right,' said Jay. 'It's a bit of a laugh.'

'Really?' said Josh.

'Yeah. Why not?'

Josh finished his sandwich.

'What now?' asked Jay.

This was a problem.

The van was full. There was nowhere to store the stuff.

Josh hadn't thought there would be so much. Or that it would be so big. He had nowhere to store it.

He explained to Jay.

'What about the Angel?' Jay said.

'Stop pissing about.'

'No. There's all sorts of buildings out the back. Used to be for horses, I think.'

Josh thought about it.

'It's worth a try,' he said.

It was perfect.

'Fifty a week,' said the landlord. 'For the lot. Cash up front.'

'Thirty,' said Josh.

'Forty.'

'Thirty,' said Josh again. 'They're empty now. It's money for nothing.'

The landlord thought about it.

'Thirty,' he said. 'And forty after six months.'

Josh shook his hand.

That night Josh slept soundly.

He was tired.

And he was happy.

Before he turned out the light he sent Lisa a text.

'2morrow. 8.30. angel. U kno it?'

The reply came instantly.

'See you there. X'

Things to think about...

Why doesn't Lisa answer her phone?

What do you think of Josh's business now? What has changed?

What difference do you think Lisa has made to Josh?

23

Clearance

———•◆•———

It was the best day of Josh's life.

Lisa looked fantastic. Jeans and boots and a jumper. And she still looked great. Her perfume filled the air.

She sat in the middle in the cab of his van.

When they got to the house she charmed the old man. She made tea and helped him pack up his own things. Josh and Jay shifted the furniture.

'I'm going into care,' said the man. 'I can't cope here.'

Lisa put her hand on his.

'We'll give you a good price for this,' she said. 'Won't we, Josh?'

There was no arguing with her.

'Course we will,' he said.

It took all morning.

The old man waved them off.

'He was nice,' said Lisa.

Jay looked out of the window.

'What do you do with the stuff?' she asked.

Josh told her about the Angel.

'And then you auction it?' she asked.

Josh hesitated.

'I suppose so,' he said. 'We push it through junk shops usually.'

'Don't they rip you off?' she asked.

'Sort of,' said Josh.

He pulled into the pub yard.

Jay opened the big doors and started making room for the new stuff.

Lisa linked her arm through Josh's.

'You know,' she said, 'I thought you might have been a crook. With the stall and everything.'

She leaned up and kissed him.

'I'm sorry,' she said.

'Look,' said Josh, 'there's something I want to tell you.'

She put her finger on his lips.

'Not now,' she said. 'If you like, I can sort out the auction room for you. You'll get a better price.'

'Yeah,' said Josh. 'Good. You do that.'

When it was all locked up he sent Jay off.

'Half day,' he said. 'I'll pay you the rest, though.'

'Sorted,' said Jay.

He went into the pub.

'Where shall we go?' asked Lisa.

'My mum will be out at bingo,' said Josh.

She kissed him again. Longer this time.

'Shall we go to your place then?' she asked.

Things to think about . . .

Do you think Josh cleaned up his business for Lisa or because of the police?

What do you think Josh wanted to say to Lisa?

Why did Josh pay Jay for a full day?

24

Women get together

———◆◆◆———

Lisa slipped out of bed and put on Josh's shirt. It just came to the top of her legs.

'I'll make some tea,' she said.

Josh reached out.

'Thanks,' he said. 'For today.'

She leaned over. The shirt fell open. Josh put his hand out.

Lisa backed away and laughed.

'I need a cup of tea,' she said.

'Afterwards,' said Josh.

She let the shirt fall to the floor and got back into bed.

'What are you like?' she smiled.

Josh kissed her.

'You're the first girl I ever brought to the house,' he said.

'I'd better be the last then,' said Lisa.

And she took over.

Afterwards, she grabbed the shirt and gave it to him.

'Now you have to make the tea,' she said.

'Can't you?'

She laughed.

'I offered. You had the chance. Now it's your turn.'

Josh pulled on trousers. He didn't bother with the shirt.

'Milk, no sugar,' said Lisa.

His mum was in the kitchen.

'I didn't hear you come in,' said Josh.

'You were busy,' she said.

She poured two cups of tea.

Josh went red.

'Is she a nice girl?' his mum asked.

'Yes. She is,' said Josh.

'Good. I'll say hello when she comes down.'

He took the tea upstairs and told Lisa.

'No?' she said. 'Sod it. What will she think?'

'It's all right,' said Josh. 'Come and meet her.'

It was all right.

They got on so well Josh felt uncomfortable.

'You'll stay and eat, won't you?' Josh's mum said.

'There's no food in,' said Josh.

He wanted Lisa out of the house.

'We'll get a take-away,' said his mum. 'You will stay, won't you?'

'I'd love to,' said Lisa.

Josh had to go out for an Indian.

It was late when Lisa left.

Josh walked her to the bus stop.

'I could drive you home,' he said. 'In the van.'

'No. This is fine,' said Lisa. 'I like your mum.'

'She likes you, too,' said Josh.

'I'd like to see her again.'

'Would you?' said Josh.

'Yes.'

'All right, then.'

Things to think about . . .

Why did Josh clear his room of stuff?

Do you think Josh's mum knew what was going on upstairs?

Why do you think Josh feels uncomfortable when Lisa gets on well with his mum?

25

Tidy

There were still a couple of things Josh had to do.

He took Mick's last cheque.

'Don't come back for more,' warned Mick. 'We're even now. Right?'

'Right,' agreed Josh.

Mick put his hand out for Josh to shake.

Josh nearly walked away. In the end he decided not to. He shook Mick's hand.

The bank took the cheque. No questions. He was legit. He had an account. Him. Josh.

There was a jeweller's two doors down from the bank.

He walked up with a smile.

The smile didn't last long. Someone should send for the police. The jeweller was a bigger robber than Josh had ever been. Those prices! Someone should put a brick through the window.

He walked away.

Half way down the street he stopped. He turned and walked back.

He bought a brooch and a bracelet.

'Would you like them gift wrapped?' the assistant asked him.

'Is it extra?'

'No. It's all in the price.'

'Go on, then,' said Josh. 'Get my money's worth.'

She smiled. But Josh didn't think she wanted to.

Just one last thing.

Josh wasn't sure how to do it. But he knew he had to.

He knew which street it was. Might as well just go and do it.

He found the house. It had a green door. He remembered stuff like that.

But he didn't know what to say.

Maybe another day. Maybe he should just forget it. It didn't matter.

He stepped back, ready to go away.

The door opened. A woman looked out at him.

She was surprised. She had her coat on. A bag in one hand and the key in the other.

'What do you want?' she said. 'I'm just going out.'

Josh gave her his best robber's smile. Cheeky.

'Hello, ma,' he said. 'Remember me?'

She looked at him.

'No.'

He bent and opened his bag. He took out an old tin.

'Remember this?' he said.

He handed it to her.

'It's my tin,' she said. 'I lost it. I've been looking for it. Everywhere.'

She hugged it to her.

'You gave it me by mistake,' said Josh. 'When I cleared your room. I brought it back.'

She was crying. Josh wanted to get away. Quick.

'Anyway,' he said, backing off.

She grabbed his arm.

'Thank you,' she said. 'You don't know what this means.'

'It's all there,' said Josh. 'Count it.'

'What?' she asked.

'The money,' he said. 'Open it.'

He helped her open the tin. It wasn't easy. She didn't want to let go of it.

'See,' said Josh.

The money covered the base of the tin.

'Four hundred and twenty pounds,' he said. 'It's all there. I counted it.'

She laughed. 'You have it,' she said.

She picked up the notes.

'What?'

'Reward,' she said. 'For bringing my tin back.'

Josh shook his head.

'No,' he said. 'It's all right.'

'It's the tin that matters,' she explained. 'It was from my husband. His first present. We didn't have much money. He saved for it. It reminds me of him. I'd forgotten the money was there. You have it. It doesn't matter. Long as I've got the tin back.'

She tried to give him the cash. He folded her old fingers around the notes.

'No,' he said. 'It's yours. Buy yourself something nice. He'd like that.'

He closed the lid on the cash.

She smiled up at him and patted his cheek.

'Thank you,' she said. 'Thank you for bringing it back.'

She had a thought.

'You could have run off with it,' she said. 'For the money.'

'Right,' agreed Josh.

'It's lovely to meet someone honest,' she said.

'Isn't it, though,' he said.

Things to think about...

How are things left between Josh and Mick?

Do you think they will see each other again?

Why does Josh buy the jewellery?

Why does Josh take the tin back to the old lady?